F.H

D1356128

MACHINE

Peter Adolphsen

Machine

TRANSLATED
FROM THE DANISH
BY

Charlotte Barslund

HARVILL SECKER LONDON

Published by Harvill Secker 2008

2 4 6 8 10 9 7 5 3 1

First published with the title *Machine* in 2006
by Samleren GB-forlagene A/S, København 2006

First published in Great Britain in 2008 by
Harvill Secker, Random House
20 Vauxhall Bridge Road
London SW1V 2SA

www.rbooks.co.uk

Addresses for companies within The Random House Group Limited can be found at:
www.randomhouse.co.uk/offices.htm

The Random House Group Limited Reg. No. 954009

A CIP catalogue record for this book is available from the British Library

ISBN 9781846551031

The Random House Group Limited supports The Forest Stewardship
Council (FSC), the leading international forest certification organisation. All our titles
that are printed on Greenpeace approved FSC certified paper carry the FSC logo. Our
paper procurement policy can be found at www.rbooks.co.uk/environment

Typeset in Adobe Caslon by Palimpsest
Book Production Limited, Grangemouth, Stirlingshire
Printed and bound in Germany by GGP Media, GmbH, Pößneck

Thank you to:
Michael Ala, Allan Hansen, Kristian Himmelstrup,
Paul Martin Holm, Karen Bonde Larsen, Litteraturrådet,
Rune Lykkeberg, Susan Metzler, Craig D. Morgan,
Mattias Pape, Arne Herløv Petersen, José Raya,
Kirsten Skjoldborg, Statens Kunstfond (especially),
Nikolaj Thyssen and Arpad A. Vass.

At 7.59 p.m. on the 23rd of June 1975 on 1st South Street in Austin, Texas, a drop of petrol combusted in a car engine. Chance would have it that the burning of this drop of fuel formed the point of intersection for the stories of the two passengers in the car as well as that of the drop itself, which had once more changed state, this time into exhaust fumes.

Time and space were once curled together to the extent that neither of them existed, but nevertheless, suddenly, somehow, a bubble appeared; an explosion occurred simultaneously everywhere and every single particle of matter separated as the void dispersed them all. As the universe continued to expand, the temperature fell sufficiently for the first elements to be formed, which they swiftly were, and thus set off a chain of metamorphoses which has continued ever since. Consequently it can be argued that all matter has always been in existence, although in various states and degrees of organisation, and has on a cosmic scale always amounted to the same quantity; nothing can be added and nothing can be subtracted. The universe is in possession of such immense quantities of matter, space and time that it is possible, through changes caused by changes, to try out endless combinations resulting in the present huge number of structures ranging from amino acids to galaxy clusters. The story of a speck of·matter is thus the story of these spontaneous structures and their altered states. The tiny element of matter which concerns us has, like everything else, existed since the Big Bang, as it is known; however, the point in time when this drop of petrol existed in its highest degree of concentration, when it entered into its most refined structure, was here on this planet fifty-five million years ago, during the early Eocene when its constituents still formed the rapidly beating heart of a small prehistoric horse. After combusting on the 23rd of June 1975, the drop acquired its most unstructured state in the form of exhaust fumes, yet managed nevertheless in this state, twenty-four hours later, to bring about a structure both complex and chaotic: cancer. I know this because I was eavesdropping from the neighbouring balcony as she inhaled the particles which triggered the pathological cell division. However, we are getting ahead of ourselves now; let us begin with the prehistoric horse.

At the end of a long hot day mist was rising from the surface of the lake. The little herd had moved down to the shore and our horse, the one with the heart in question, a five-year-old mare, could feel her fear of crocodiles constricting her throat. She wedged herself in between two of the other horses and stuck her muzzle out across the fragmented mirror surface; she secured her footing and drank, with a sigh, at last.

The animal was a mammal of the Perissodactyla order, the Equidae family, best known as *Eohippus*, the dawn horse, as it was named by Othniel C. Marsh in 1876; however, as Richard Owen had already in 1841 named a certain fossil *Hyracotherium*, the rules of taxonomy dictated that this term was the correct one. Owen had missed the link with the domestic horse and believed that the animal was related to the shrewmouse, the Latin name for which is *Hyrax*. Common aesthetic sense has since ensured that this name, both prettier and more appropriate, is most frequently used, usually listed first, or if not, then following in brackets. *Eohippus* is often compared to a fox terrier, partly because they are similar in size, but also because the point of this breed was to create a dog in the image of a horse. During a hunt the terrier sits on the saddle and it was considered tasteful if the rider/dog owner had a small simulacrum of his own horse that could continue the hunt underground. At dog shows it was therefore regarded as a plus if a dog's coat had markings in the shape of a saddle.

Our five-year-old mare in the early Eocene, whose coat was a speckled grey-brown, felt a sudden surge of anxiety as the image of a *Diatryma*, a bird of prey more than two metres in height without any wings to speak of, but consequently with far bigger thighs, claws and beak, surfaced in her mind. She raised her head and noticed in the reflection of the water how the hairs on her muzzle quivered, made static by the electricity in the air.

'What?' she wondered.

Convection wind caused the day's evaporation to rise until it was halted by the chill from the outer atmosphere and condensed into cumulonimbus clouds. The turbulence within the clouds shattered rain, hail and ice, producing smaller, electrically

4

charged particles. The disparity in voltage between the surface of the earth and the clouds rapidly approached the number of millions of volts per cubic metre that would trigger a spark. The hairs on our *Eohippus*'s little body stood on end as she sensed the electricity in the air. In an instant a bolt of lightning shot its plasma cord deep into the forest, barely one hundred metres away from the horses, and the resulting crash of thunder was so loud that they were temporarily struck deaf. The sudden silence in their heads contributed to their panic. Billions of synapses flashed in the horses' brains as their autonomous nervous system took control of their bodies and triggered an automatic fright-flee response. The direction of flight was initially diametrically opposite to the light and the sound.

The horse's heart instantly obeyed the command from the sympathetic nervous system: noradrenaline in generous quantities stimulated the sinus node in order to increase the frequency of impulses that ran down through the atrioventricular node, then separated at the bundle of His into the right and left branches and caused, with appropriate delays in the right places, the muscle fibres to demand an ever-increasing working rate from the heart. The alternating contractions and relaxations of the heart muscles allowed blood in regulated quantities to flow into the right atrium, onwards to the right ventricle and from there out into the lungs, where it released carbon dioxide and absorbed oxygen; thereafter the blood flowed to the left atrium of the heart, down into the left ventricle and through the aorta out into the body. The heart's rhythm accelerated; its muscles and the brain demanding fresh blood.

The horses ran along the lakeshore, but soon darted into the undergrowth of the forest, where the darkness was even denser now the clouds had compressed. Underneath her somewhat rasping breathing the mare could hear her blood pump through her ears.

Rain followed shortly afterwards, first as light showers, which they hardly noticed, growing heavier and then a sudden cloudburst. Gusts of wind swept curtains of heavy drops across the treetops and the surface of the lake. The horses continued their flight through the storm, until an element of indecision began to characterise their movements. Our mare chose the wrong path around a fallen tree and was lagging behind the herd; she could see the two horses in front of her jump over a swelling brook, whereas the third one had halted. She hesitated: disorientated she was able neither to stop nor jump and consequently fell into the muddy water with a splash. For a while she fought to keep her head above water, but the current got hold of her and dragged her downwards. Then she banged her head against a rock and lost consciousness.

It would appear to be the shimmering sunlight creeping in under the rim of her eyelids which made the mare wake up, and not the crow sitting on her thigh pecking at a wound. Our mare, who was dazed but alive, jerked to scare the bird away, but experienced in the very same second a threatening loss of balance as a void opened up beneath her. It was not until now that she realised where she was: on a tangled mass of roots protruding from a steep slope that fell away down towards the lake a terrifying distance below her. A huge tree stooped over the slope and its voluminous network of roots, partly revealed by the rain, had broken her fall towards certain death in the lake. It was an ancient maple, more than thirty metres tall, whose roots stuck out ten metres into the air. The horse gingerly shifted her weight to a more secure footing, stood up and checked herself: there was a gash on her thigh, she was generally bruised and a sharp pain throbbed in her temple, but no broken bones it would seem. She made it up the tangled roots towards the edge of the slope on hesitant legs, but the last bit necessitated a small jump which she prepared for but ultimately did not dare attempt.

'Wait until tomorrow,' she thought and stretched her neck out for some leaves. She was not short of drinking water either as the brook, now reduced to a small stream, cascaded from the slope and flowed through the roots down into the lake while making a constant trickling sound. Having quenched her thirst and eaten most of what she could reach, she found a broad root to settle down on.

'This is safe,' she thought. 'Crocodile cannot reach up. *Diatryma* cannot reach down.'

The sun set and the moon rose. For a long time the mare lay there looking alternately at the moon and its reflection in the surface of the water. Finally she decided that the moon must have a sister who lived in the lake. She whinnied contentedly at this explanation, fell asleep and dreamed that she was watching dust particles dance in a beam of sunlight. A column of ants marched past her on the forest floor. Suddenly, with incredible speed, the whiskers on her muzzle grew into long, heavy, quivering rods that bashed into tree trunks and branches whenever she tried to move. Every time a whisker hit something a shrill note rang out in her skull. This quickly escalated into a cacophony that was approaching her pain threshold . . . which was when the dream ended, before the mare had time to surface from her sleep.

This period of sleep gave the animal's organism the chance to concentrate on the healing process which had commenced within seconds of her sustaining her injuries. First the body tried to cleanse its wounds of impurities and dead tissue by allowing white blood corpuscles to emigrate from the bloodstream out into the tissue, where the neutrophil granulocytes carried out a number of functions, such as fagocytosis and the excretion of enzymes to break down tissue and bacteria. The product of this process, inflammatory exudate, was now gradually turning into granulation tissue though angiogenesis and fibroblast proliferation: the wound was forming a scab.

Throughout the night another process persevered: the seepage from the brook and the considerable weight of the maple, together with the mare's small, but nevertheless crucial weight, eroded the slope, which eventually gave way round about midnight. A huge chunk of soil crashed into the lake with a rumble and a splash, and these noises roused the horse out of her sleep, but, before she had time to look around, the tree, with a deep groan, tilted 30° whereupon the horse lost her footing and tumbled towards the water, landing first on a small floating island formed from a chunk of the collapsed slope. During the few seconds that passed before the temporary vessel sank, the mare had time to smell the newly upturned soil and watch the tree keel over so it hung diagonally downwards. What were formerly the top branches now dangled just beyond her reach. Simultaneously the unstable ground beneath her gave way. Another splash. Wide-eyed she struggled for just under a minute, but then gave up. The mud on the bottom enveloped the little horse almost lovingly. Her final thought concerned the taste of fern shoots.

Death exists, but only in a practical, macroscopic sense. Biologically one cannot distinguish between life and death; the transition is a continuum. Furthermore, at this point nature consists of irreducible processes rather than clearly defined categories. The problem of defining death mirrors a corresponding difficulty with the definition of life: a living organism is formed of non-living material, organised so it can absorb energy to maintain its system, and death is thus the irreversible cessation of these functions. However, this definition feels too simplistic since the extent to which and how a system should be organised in order to be described as living, and precisely what aspects of its functions need to cease before death can be considered as having occurred, will always depend on an estimate. Besides, according to this definition certain sea anemones that reproduce through asexual division are immortal; as are bacteria, which merely replicate themselves as the old cells perish – which, incidentally, is a stroke of luck for us, as the globe would otherwise be covered by a metre-thick layer of them within a matter of days. However, we mammals are not distracted by the relationship that bacteria and sea anemones have with death; instinctively we know that death occurs when the heart stops beating – but even that is merely an illusion: partly because the heart can be kept pumping after all brain activity has ceased, partly because the majority of cells in the body continue to live a period of time after the heart has stopped, and finally because the death of any major organism means the start of a veritable explosion of another, primarily bacterial, form of life.

The chain of transformation continues indefinitely; precisely how depends on the actual circumstances and in this instance – our horse at the bottom of the lake – the change of state occurred anaerobically as mire and mud completely enveloped the animal. A few minutes after the heart had stopped beating, the cytoplasm of the muscle cells solidified to a gel due to the accumulation of lactic acid from the heart's failed attempt to pump without oxygen. The blood, saturated by carbon dioxide, stopped circulating and flowed towards the lowest parts of the cadaver where haemoglobin seeped into the surrounding tissue and began to appear as dark spots beneath the skin under the speckled coat. The small body emitted its heat to the mire and was soon in balance with the temperature of its surroundings, approximately 9° Celsius. Various enzymes associated with the decomposition and breakdown functions of living tissue took advantage of their newly found freedom to instigate an internal dissolution of cells until these exploded and released their highly nutritious contents. Enzyme-rich organs, such as the stomach and the pancreas, and watery organs, such as the brain, were the first to be attacked. The decomposition resulted in the creation of air in the soft parts of the animal; the liver and the brain were quickly transformed into a foam-like structure with tiny, closely positioned blisters. Once the contents of the decomposed cells were added, it was time for micro-organisms – bacteria, fungi and protozoa from the airways, the stomach and especially the intestines – to carry out the actual putrefaction. At breakneck speed they broke down tissue into fluids such as indole, scatole, putrescine, cadaverine, as well as a range of fatty acids, while simultaneously forming gases such as methane, ammoniac, hydrogen sulphide, sulphur dioxide and carbon dioxide. An incalculable throng of minute existences participated in this explosive activity and what follows is merely an incomplete list of the strains of bacteria present: *Acinetobacter, Actinobacillus, Butyrivibrio, Clostridium, Desulfotomaculum, Desulfovibrio, Enterobacter, Escherichia, Fusobacterium, Methanobacterium, Methanococcus, Moraxella, Nitrosomona, Proteus, Salmonella, Thiobacillus, Vibrio* and *Zymomona.* A metropolis of microscopic beings were created in the deceased horse and, in the course of time, they converted its soft parts into a viscous, green-black mass of bacteria busy eating their dead parentage. The bones retained their state for a while, but eventually they too succumbed and began to dissolve.

Layer upon layer of material was deposited at the bottom of the lake as time passed; over millions of years the patient micrometres of sediments became kilometres of strata on top of the heart of the small *Eohippus*. The pressure from the multiple tonnes of material, the heat from the earth's core and the general heaving and nudging of the landscape in the form of shifts, folds and faults eventually broke down the decayed remains of the horse into oil or more precisely, a vast amount of hydrocarbon bonds, variations on the basal structure $C_{(x)}H_{(2x+2)}$.

The lake and the forest had long since disappeared and been replaced by arid mountains intersected by rivers. The slowly forming oil meandered through the surrounding minerals and accumulated in pockets – collectively known as the Green River Formation, once oil in serious quantities was discovered in the area in 1948. The small quantity of oil that had once been the heart of a mare, was now located just under one kilometre below ground level, thirteen kilometres south of the town of Jensen. The area was called the Uinta Basin and belonged to the federal state of Utah in the United States of America.

The darkness and the silence of underground were broken one day in 1973 when the 3 x 3 slanted, individually rotating, toothed rims of a drilling crown carved their way to the oil pocket. Under high pressure, water was injected down into the borehole, forcing oil up to the surface where it was transferred through a pipeline to Chevron's refinery in Salt Lake City. At the very moment when our drop of oil was on its way through the pipeline at Walker Hollow an accident occurred there, which cost a worker his lower right arm.

At the time in question this worker called himself Jimmy Nash, but his original name was Djamolidine Hasanov. He was born in 1948, the only child of Hosni, an oil worker, and Ivana, a shop assistant in the local Produkty; both were Kumyks and residents of Baku, the capital of Azerbaijani SSR. When Djamolidine was ten years old two things occurred which were to shape his future destiny: he was given a racer bike, and the Central Commission for Statistics of the Soviet Union carried out a national census. His father had miraculously conjured up the bike: a brand new Velosipedov with genuine rubber tyres, perforated leather saddle, drop handlebars, toe brackets on the pedals and hand brakes. The frame was pillar-box red with a yellow hammer and sickle on the head tube. From this day onwards Djamolidine spent as much time as possible in the saddle; school lessons were spent pining for the Velosipedov and, as soon as he got home, he would scamper down the stairwell of their block of flats with his bike slung across his shoulder, leap onto the saddle and race around until just before sunset. It was a rule that he had to be back in time for evening prayers and there were no exceptions.

Djamolidine's parents were a tad more religious than most people in Baku and insisted that all three members of the family – Hosni, Ivana and Djamolidine – joined in the daily prayers at sunrise and sunset as well as the noon prayer on Fridays. Also, pork and alcohol were rarely allowed inside the door of their allocated flat, which consisted of three rooms plus a bathroom with a sit-in bathtub. Apart from that Djamolidine was free to do whatever he wanted outside in the officially atheist country. He wanted to ride his bike.

He followed the various roads out of town towards Siazan, Maraza or Alyat. He crisscrossed areas with flamboyant houses, once the homes of rich people in pre-revolutionary times and now the oil districts. There thousands of drilling towers soared, making up a kind of anti-forest complete with abandoned and producing wells to represent dead and living trees respectively, and anti-lakes in the form of oil pools with hardened surfaces. Flares, rusty oil barrels, damaged drill pipes and drilling crowns and a range of abandoned machinery assumed the character of animals and bushes. On Saturdays Djamolidine always brought a packed lunch out to the drilling operation where his father was working. Every week he cut a couple of seconds off the time it took him to ride this distance.

Nature had blessed Djamolidine with a photographic memory for lists and registers; for example he could reel off the contents page of the popular edition of Lenin's writings, including pagination, or the Shiite line of imams from Ali up until the present day, including Islamic as well as Christian calendar dates. He soon memorised the names and the order of the road signs for the various routes he took and would, on his way home, recite them out loud or simply visualise them in his head, even spelling their names backwards as he cycled past.

One afternoon, as he was riding very slowly in order to improve his balance, a Lada pulled in on the square in front of his apartment block. The emblem on the bonnet indicated that it belonged to the Central Commission for Statistics for the Soviet Union. It was a well-known fact that a national census was being carried out this year. One of his school friends owned a sheet of stamps which depicted a census official, an apparatchik in a nice tie, visiting a range of Soviet people: Russians, Mongolians, Turks etc. All the stamps showed the same dark blond official, as a result of which Djamolidine, perhaps subconsciously, had imagined that all census officials would look like that, but his illusions were shattered when the car door opened and a wheezing, black-haired dumpling of a man got out. The two of them briefly made eye contact, the fat man and the boy on his bike, whereupon the official plodded in the direction of the first stairwell. There was a blotch of sweat on the back of his shirt.

When there was a knock on their door four hours later, the family was ready, their hair wet combed and everyone holding their identity papers. The flat was in the top corner of the block and was consequently the twelfth and final stop on today's list for 'comrade Boris Zverev, senior assistant from SCKS' as he introduced himself. He was clearly in no hurry to leave and only made a brief show of turning down the offer of a cup of tea. Having processed the registration of the family, Zverev made himself even more comfortable on the sofa with a fresh cup of tea and said:

'Even though a census is and indeed should be the epitome of exact, factual truth – one, two, three is an indisputable sequence, isn't it? – there exists a degree of uncertainty both before and after the census, and that is in choosing *what* to count to begin with and how to *interpret* the results afterwards. Both these elements are the antithesis to numbers: selection and interpretation are activities which presume an acting subject, a human being, and all human beings are fallible. However, here in the Soviet Union we are fortunate that the state apparatus, in this instance the Interior Ministry, employs the most refined and rational science to compute these two tasks for us. The principles behind this census . . .'

At this point Zverev placed his briefcase on his lap and began looking for some documents, but stopped halfway to add: 'Our task is to count the people, who broadly speaking can be defined on the basis of whatever language they speak. But when is a language a language and not merely a dialect? In real life there are plenty of hybrid and transitional forms, and yet the vast majority speak a clearly defined language. Languages are a product of the dynamics of history. History passes through a series of phases, as you well know, from the hunter-gatherer stage on to feudalism to capitalism, socialism and finally communism. Language development likewise progresses in parallel phases, which are also characterised by an increasing rationality in their construction. After all, we live in the imperfect socialist period where language differences still exist. However, with the arrival of communism, and this is my personal theory, people will naturally, because they are equal men and women of intertwined cultures, acquire a common language, which for historical reasons will be Russian.'

He said that in Russian. A moment's silence followed. Zverev, peering around the spartanly furnished living room and then remembering that his hand was halfway down his briefcase, twitched slightly and pulled out the desired piece of paper.

'The peoples of the Soviet Union of Socialist Republics are initially divided into nine groups: Slavs, Finno-Ugrics, Turks, Mongolians, Iranians, Ibero-Caucasians, Latins, Germanics, and Latvian-Lithuanians.' At this point he turned to consult the paper: 'The following are Slavs: Russians, Ukrainians, White Russians, Poles, and Bulgarians. The following are Finno-Ugrics: Estonians, Mordvins, Karelians, Udmurts (formerly known as Votiaks), Maris, Hungarians, Finns, Komi Zyrians and Komi Permyaks. The Turkic peoples are Uzbeks, Tatars, Kazakhs, Azerbaijanis, Chuvashes, Turkmen, Bashkirs, Kyrgyzs, Yakuts, Karakalpaks and Kumyks,' – here he threw a quick glance at the family – 'Tuvins, Gagauses, Uigurs, Karachays, Khakassins, Altaians, Balkars, Nogais and Crimean Tartars. Mongolians are Buryats, Kalmyks and Koreans. The Iranian peoples are made up of Armenians (often counted as a people in their own right, but not in this census), Tajiks, North Ossetians, South Ossetians and Greeks. The Ibero-Caucasian peoples are Georgians, Chechens, Ingushes, Avars, Tsezs (who speak the same language), Adyghes, and Abazars. The Latin peoples are Romanians and Moldavians (who also speak Romanian, but use the Cyrillic alphabet).

Germanic peoples are Germans and Yiddish-speaking Jews. Latvian-Lithuanians are, as their name implies, Latvians and Lithuanians. Apart from that there is an appendix concerning Nenets (formerly known as Samoyeds), Veps, Kriashens, Besermyans, Tungus, Telenganas, Kashgars, Talyshes and Yedysans.'

The family members had not taken in a great deal of Zverev's first statement; the list of peoples, however, made a huge impression on Djamolidine. The geographic outline of the Soviet Union swirled like a spiral galaxy in his mind as the size of the country finally began to sink in.

Shortly afterwards Hosni politely escorted Zverev to the door and Ivana sent Djamolidine to bed. Later, as the boy lay in the darkness, he imagined the swell of all the languages in the world spoken simultaneously.

From that day onwards Djamolidine kept a notebook in his pocket where he would write an entry every time he met a person from a different people. He quickly reached twenty-five different ones and then thirty, but at that point his interest began to fade or, rather, his frustration with the existing system of classification grew, while simultaneously his own attempt at creating a superior one started running into difficulties: for example, should there be specific subcategories for people of mixed race; a boy at his school had grandparents who were Armenian, Azerbaijani, Russian and German respectively, and so ought he to have his own particular subclass? Which would be a subcategory of what precisely? He considered classification according to mother tongue, but that would produce misleading results – for himself, for example, who was Kumyk, but spoke and thought in Russianised Azerbaijani. Nor would religion or geography be workable parameters for classification. Everything can be divided into more and more categories the closer you look at it, he thought, and vice versa, every single phenomenon ticks several boxes when you look at the bigger picture. Likewise there are several names for every single object. Take him, for instance: his full name was Djamolidine Hasanov, but his friends and family normally called him Djamo, and his mother sometimes called him Moli or just Mo. His schoolteacher called him Young Pioneer Hasanov, and in the playground he was known as Djimi or Rat, if anyone wanted to tease him. As a cyclist he wanted to be known as the Vulture from Baku. In addition, everything could be written using different symbols. The three generations in Djamolidine's family each used a different alphabet: he himself used Cyrillic for writing in Russian and Azerbaijani, his father, Hosni, however, had learned the Latin alphabet in school and wrote in Azerbaijani sprinkled with numerous Russian words and certain Kumyk adaptations. Finally there was Nusrat, his grandfather, who had learned Persian and Arabic at a madrasa in Tabriz before the revolution, and now in his old age used the Arabic alphabet in order to produce a form of Kumyk spelling of his own invention. Both Hosni and Nusrat were able to read Cyrillic letters, but they did not use them for writing. Djamolidine was particularly mesmerised by his grandfather's flourishes.

In time the contents of the notebook underwent a barely discernible shift from data collection to musings, which orbited around a basic piece of knowledge he acquired the evening the censor visited them: the world is huge. It triggered a longing to travel abroad, which for the time being could be relieved by the sucking sound of rubber tyres against tarmac.

Power is a measure of an individual's or an institution's ability to influence others in order to achieve its own goals. This involves two things: will and the ability to enforce one's will, if necessary, by violent means. Only rarely is actual physical force applied, as the implied threat, paired with a clear allocation of roles, generally encourages the weaker part to surrender in advance, frequently without the parties themselves even becoming aware of this process. Power play is the prevailing way for states as well as individuals to behave and is consequently the cement that enables relationships between various entities to be maintained; a kind of existential connective tissue. Power exists in political, economic, sociological, psychological and other situations and the tendency to create structures, through which power can be exercised, can be found everywhere. The larger the power the more complex the structures.

When Djamolidine in 1962, aged fourteen years and motivated by his desire to take part in competitive cycling, became a member of Komsomol, he joined at one of the lowest levels of what is probably the most complex power structure ever created: the state formation known as the Union of Socialist Soviet Republics. This structure was, despite a relentlessly proclaimed equality, hierarchical as few had ever been: at the top was the general secretary and below him the state apparatus with the Ministerial Council, the Supreme Soviet and its Presidium, the Soviet of the Union and the Soviet of Nationalities, the Ministerial Councils of the fifteen republics and the Supreme Soviet, the Soviets of the approximately 150 regions with their associated executive committees and below them the Soviet and executive committees of approximately 5,600 districts and 45,000 villages. All authorities were officially elected from the bottom up, but in reality were appointed from the top by the Communist Party which represented the heart, spinal column and peripheral nerves in a triangular structure consisting of a bureau, a committee and a secretariat – a structure which replicated itself up through the levels of the pyramid starting with local party associations, to districts and regions, to republics and at the very top the Polit Bureau, the Central Committee and the Secretariat of the Central Committee. The military and the police forces, with or without uniform, were the muscles of the structure, and the education systems and various cultural institutions acted as the intestines. In addition there were trade unions, women's organisations, artists' unions, the pioneer organisations for children and the aforementioned organisation for young people, Komsomol.

Having been admitted into his local division, Djamolidine was accepted into a Baku cycling team and was soon afterwards promoted to the Autonomous Soviet Socialist Republic's under-16s team as there was no shortage of his talent or motivation. He quickly grasped that the sport of cycling involved much more than merely pedalling uphill on a metal frame with rubber wheels. The presence of other riders turned his attempts to reduce wind resistance into a relentless game. He realised the importance of reading the wheel of the rider in front of him, following the rhythm; he experienced being sucked into a field of possibly a hundred riders, cycling in a fan formation to cancel out the wind and forming part of a breakaway group of leads. When he had been cycling on his own he had been playing a simple game of three-in-a-row; now it was chess or Go.

His coaches tried to make him cycle laps, but Djamolidine despised this repetitive pedalling that got him nowhere and deliberately rode below his ability.

'I'm a mountain biker!' he stated, making a defiant stance with his skinny, but sinewy body.

His teenage years passed with school, training and races for the ASSR team, where he now only just managed to be promoted to the under-18s and did not even come close to being selected for the national youth team, and he was able to hold on to his place purely because he had swallowed even more amphetamines than his competitors at the qualifying races. His talent was, in other words, limited. His life away from cycling was becoming increasingly unfocused and, when the time came for a possible promotion to the senior teams, everyone involved already knew what the answer would be.

In the period that followed he tried with diminishing ardour to find work as a bicycle mechanic. At home the respect he had once commanded started to fade away as he was no longer seen wearing the colours of the national team, and, in the absence of cycling training camps, he began to feel seriously trapped in his parents' flat. He tried going out for daylong rides in the mountains, but riding on his own was and always would be a poor substitute.

Both his parents and the authorities made it clear that finding a job was now a priority and Djamolidine finally saw no alternative to the oil industry. He was hired as a tapper on a state drilling operation. After two and a half years, however, he had become sufficiently fed up with staring at the slow see-sawing counter-weight movements of the pumps to carry out an idea which had been forming in his mind for a long time: escaping from the republic.

He would ride his bike across the mountains to Iran in order to apply for asylum at the American embassy in Teheran. The majority of the border between Azerbaijani SSR and Iran followed the Arak River. However, towards the south and out towards the coast, the border went through the Talesh Mountains and Djamolidine had heard of a path which would take him as far as the border. As long as he succeeded in getting across the border, he would be able to find his way on the other side easily.

Once he had completed his preparations his backpack contained the following: one change of clothes in a waterproof bag, identity papers and other documents, one hundred roubles and a little Iranian currency (a 500-rial note and a few coins), a water bottle and ten herbal biscuits wrapped in waxed paper together with a bolt cutter. He was wearing his national cycling team outfit with black weatherproofs on the outside.

On the evening of the 27th of October 1970, a

northerly wind was blowing. At midnight he tiptoed out of the flat, leaving a brief letter explaining to his parents that he would miss them, but that his desire to see the Western world was too great.

The darkness, the rain, the tailwind and the black garments aided him. He was possibly aided by Allah as well; Djamolidine was not entirely sure if he still believed in him, but as he headed for the border, he did catch himself thinking about the Gracious and the Merciful. Or he might just have been unbelievably lucky: he encountered no officials, Soviet or Iranian, the fences were few and the barbed wire rusty. Nor was the cold any worse than could be offset by the physical exertion.

At dawn, after resting, he got back on the saddle and made his way down the mountains into Iran. The skies began to clear as he approached a town which he, with his superficial knowledge of the Persian seriffed Arabic alphabet, could decipher as 'Ardabil'. Sheltered by the sign, he took a break, changed his clothes, ate, drank and loosened up his muscles before getting back onto his bike, and he did not get off it until he reached Teheran eighteen hours later. The exultation and the lack of sleep induced in him a sensation of being the perfect cycling machine: the pumping action of his lungs and thigh muscles, his eyes and brain reading the road, his thorax muscle contracting rhythmically as he clenched the handlebars.

The embassy staff in Teheran, personified by a 32-year-old secretary with the remarkable name of James Stewart, was obliging almost to the point of embarrassment; the fact that Djamolidine was in possession of a domestic Soviet passport plus written evidence of participation in an elite sport, together with his stated wish to seek political asylum, meant that Section 19 of the Immigration Act applied, and Djamolidine was issued with F1-type personal papers. Hurrah.

Outside the embassy gates Djamolidine had reeled off three homemade sentences in English: 'I name Djamolidine Hasanov. I from Baku, Union of Soviets. I look to political asylum in States of America.' Taking this as his starting point he began learning the English language with an almost insatiable enthusiasm. His future would unfold in this language; he must transform himself into an American as quickly as possible – a resolution in which James Stewart was only too pleased to assist. James found him a textbook with the ambiguous title *This Way – American English for Foreigners* and changed, at Djamolidine's request, the name on the F1 papers to 'Jimmy Nash'. From now on he was Jimmy, Jimmy Nash with an extended, yankee-drawling 'a', and would never let anyone call him anything else.

A week later he was on the morning flight to Washington. He registered no special feeling when stepping on to American soil for the first time, probably because he had in effect already arrived on US territory when they let him through the gates of the embassy in Teheran.

Upon his arrival he was housed in an 'economy' motel situated by one of Washington's southern approach roads, where he spent a month watching television, teaching himself English from his textbook, and eavesdropping on people's conversations in the motel restaurant, as well as going for long walks in the anti-pedestrian shambles of the city's arterial roads. Eventually, the winter weather and a feeling of wanderlust prompted him to call James Stewart, who was delighted to 'pull a few strings' and bring about the following arrangement: Jimmy got a second-hand car – a 1964 Pontiac Strato Chief – $500 and a job contract which stipulated that two months later, on the 1st of March 1971, he would start work as a tapper at an oil well in Utah. From that date onwards he would be regarded as having been settled in America. He was free to pick his own route to Utah and, having thought about it and having been persuaded by the glittering leaflets from the US Department of Tourism, he chose to drive to Los Angeles via New Orleans, up to San Francisco and back into the country to Utah.

Fourteen days later he checked into a motel outside Charlotte, North Carolina. He stuck his key into a ball-shaped door handle and opened up the door. A wave of stale air poured out, so he crossed the small room to open a window. A piece of chocolate on the pillow appeared in his peripheral field of vision and caused a smile twinned with a tinge of tristesse to flicker across his face.

'I love America,' he whispered to himself, as he pulled out a wad of notes from his pocket and sat down on the bed. He had $200 stitched into his jacket and another $200 hidden underneath the front seat of his car and $27 in total in his hand. The chocolate on his pillow was a Hershey Bar.

Perhaps the two most striking aspects about Americans were, first, their relationship with money and branded products, and how brands were expressed pictorially, which was what advertising ultimately was. Billboards were the most prominent features of the urban environment or along the wide Interstate Highways, like this one, number 85, that he had been following for 241 miles. This forest of billboards seemed never-ending to him. The Soviet Union, too, had her propaganda signs along the lines of: 'Socialist Nations of the World March Together Towards a Marxist-Leninist Victory!', but the American slogans had rather more catchy appeal. Jimmy had amused himself by pairing off the billboards, for instance when Betty Crocker Cookies were followed by Monsieur Jorgen Diet Pills, or when Carrier Bonds Home Loans preceded U-Haul Moving Trucks.

Next to the billboards, poverty was the second most striking aspect. He had spotted early on that the presence of homeless and severely impoverished people was greatest in the city centres. However, the vast majority of the country's population lived in infinitely replicating suburban squares known as 'the grid', where the areas ranged from opulent to shabby, but each plot was sizeable compared to accommodation in Azerbaijan and invariably there was a car in the drive.

The number of overweight people was conspicuous too. If you followed the billboards' advice a little too uncritically, Jimmy thought, you would end up weighing more than two hundred pounds. He was consciously making an effort to switch to American measuring units: even in his mind he thought in ounces, gallons, inches, yards, miles etc. However, it was with considerable difficulty that he let go of the somewhat more logical systems of the old world and he never managed it completely. In unguarded moments and in dreams he still used metre and kilo.

The following day he picked up a hitchhiker: a hippie guy in his twenties, a fast-talking type as a result of which Jimmy only caught fragments of what he was saying; however, he eventually managed to piece the man's story together. His name was Butch Pozzi, he came from Rhode Island where he had worked for a while in a chocolate factory after finishing high school before being drafted to Vietnam, where he was lucky enough to do duty as a driver in the supply troops. Since then he had hung out mostly, but had recently spent six months in Europe, some of it in London, but mainly Amsterdam. His time abroad had clearly influenced his perception of himself, in particular his meeting with a certain Bart Hughes. The word 'trepanation' cropped up several times in connection with this Hughes character and Jimmy eventually had to interrupt Butch's flow of words to ask him what it meant.

'Drilling a hole in your head, man,' Butch replied, miming holding a screw auger to his forehead. The reason for performing such a bizarre procedure was apparently to create subpressure inside the skull and thus increase the flow of blood to the brain, which would result in a permanent 'high', similar to the sensation you experience after a headstand. It was all in the book which Butch pulled out of his rucksack, written by Bart Hughes himself in 1962: *Homo Sapiens Correctus (the mechanism of brainbloodvolume)*. The hippie leafed through the book for some time, while he expanded on why gravity is our enemy. Back in ancient times, when our ancestors got up to walk on two legs, we began to experience a shortage of blood to our brains. Consequently we only use ten per cent of our brain capacity because the brain does not receive enough blood – that is, nourishment. Butch did headstands every morning and was considering opting for trepanation himself, but it was just totally impossible to find the right surgeon and he didn't dare do it himself, plus it was expensive and hard to track down the right equipment. Some day maybe.

During his monologue Butch had pulled out a small bag of dried plant material and asked for permission to roll a joint, which he now lit and passed on to Jimmy.

'Great zootie, eh?' Butch asked and Jimmy, his lungs filling with smoke, nodded without understanding the actual word which, in any case, undoubtedly referred to the joint. Drug-user slang had to be one of the most changeable linguistic phenomena, he thought. Zootie.

Butch was only going as far as Chattanooga, Tennessee, where he knew some acid heads on a houseboat. Jimmy continued onwards on his own. He listened to jazz in New Orleans, gambled in a Las Vegas casino, strolled down the Los Angeles boulevards and smoked pot in a San Francisco park. And so on until he arrived at Jensen, Utah, on the 28th of February 1971.

Utah is characterised by two things: a range of crude oil and gas industries with their associated boom–bust cycles and the continuing presence of

Mormons since proselytes of this apocalyptic variant of Protestantism founded the state capital, Salt Lake City, in 1847. Today the Church of Jesus Christ of Latter-Day Saints, as they are known, has approximately ten million members and acts in every respect as a multinational corporation. The church was founded in 1830 by Joseph Smith Jr., the 25-year-old son of a poor man from Palmyra, New York. Shortly afterwards he published *The Book of Mormon*, a dense work based on a fable, which enjoyed widespread popular appeal in nineteenth-century America and which claimed that the continent was originally populated by immigrant Jews. At the beginning of the book a 'Testimony of the Prophet Joseph Smith' is given, wherein he narrates how these holy writings, engraved on a series of gold tablets, were given to him by a luminous angel who entrusted him with the translation of the 'Reformed Egyptian' language of the text into English. For this task the angel gave him a pair of silver spectacles with two jewels for lenses. The texts, which in style and appearance are reminiscent of biblical ones, tell the story of two Jewish tribes, the Jaredites and the Nefites, their exodus from Palestine to America, the evolution of their civilisation etc., and culminate with Jesus, no less, who, after his resurrection, appears to the Nefites to found God's Kingdom on earth, before ascending to Heaven for good. Once the translation had been completed, the angel came back for the gold tablets and the spectacles, as a result of which Smith, in the absence of any physical evidence, found himself forced to add statements from eleven individuals in total, all of whom were his family or close friends, who in the name of God and Jesus confirmed that they had personally seen the gold tablets with the cryptic characters. A number of contemporary sources for *The Book of Mormon* are easily identified: the King James Bible, whose vocabulary can be found everywhere; Ethan Smith's 1825 novel *View of the Hebrews*, with the subtitle: *Designed to prove among other things that the Aborigines of America are descended from the Ten Tribes of Israel*; Josiah Priest's *The Wonder of Nature and Providence* (also 1825) and an unpublished script of a novel from 1809 by Solomon Spaulding, which we know Joseph Smith had access to.

The second feature of Utah is the aforementioned underground content of valuable metals, hydrocarbons etc., and people's enthusiasm for digging them up. In the beginning Brigham Young, who succeeded Joseph Smith as prophet and head of the Mormon church with its associated access to continuous revelations, forbade his followers to search for riches in the earth and the rivers because a gold rush would attract non-Mormons or gentiles and all the sinful behaviour they would bring with them – and anyway, it was their holy duty to cultivate the desert. However, there was no stopping progress, nor could the contents of the mountains be spirited away, and the Mormons – who have always displayed a sound, capitalist pragmatism – adapted, and controlled at the turn of the century the majority of the Utah mining activities, which included the extraction of gold, silver, copper, lead, zinc and coal. There was even a rush for dinosaur bones in 1909. Later, uranium and military industries would prove to be important sources of income in addition to oil.

Needless to say, the oil was not discovered for a very long time, even though scattered signs, such as seepage from the rocks by the salt lake and along the San Juan River and the Green River, gave promise of future findings. Apart from minor isolated wells – the result of countless test drills – oil extraction in Utah did not reach a commercial scale until the 18th of September 1948 when the local Equity Oil Company in Ashley Valley in the Uinta Basin hit a stratum that yielded around three hundred barrels a day. The following years many of the big players in the industry – Standard Oil, Continental, Gulf, Carter, Exxon, Union Oil and others – opened the oil complexes Greater Altamont/Bluebell and Greater Red Wash. The job contract in the glove compartment of Jimmy's Pontiac was between him and a certain Carl Hartfield, managing director at the Walker Hollow oil field in the northern end of the Red Wash area.

The oil deposits in this area, the Green River (Eocene) Formation as it is known, are found in disc-shaped pockets in places where the folds are gentle and the faults almost non-existent. The slate layers are thoroughly compressed. Together these conditions indicate limited migration from source layer to reservoir layer. The product of the metamorphosis of a tiny horse's heart had lain almost completely undisturbed for fifty-five million years.

Jimmy quickly settled into the routine at Walker Hollow: work from 8 a.m. till 6 p.m. every day for three weeks followed by one week's holiday, which he mainly spent binge drinking in Jensen, Roosevelt, Duchesne or Provo. The small towns and their bars all looked the same. The clientele always consisted of the same four clearly defined groups: oil workers like himself, soldiers and other staff from Dugway Proving Ground, Native American Indians from the Ouray Reservation and locals who had dropped out but never managed to leave the area. The still faithful Mormons were rarely seen.

Workday evenings he spent on his own in his cabin-like room where he worked his way through *This Way 2* and its accompanying exercise booklet. In addition he also read comics about superheroes and detective stories in instalments, as well as working his way through popular novelists such as Harold Robbins, Grace Metalious and Leon Uris. The reading material was supplied by Exxon Oil Library Service, whose somewhat peculiar content made up his literary horizon. His evening reading also included two porn magazines whose overexposed photos of moist and shiny genitalia in full action aroused in him lust mixed with a tantalising undercurrent of revulsion, though it was a way of passing the time.

Working on the pump was also an effective way to kill time. He was just 24-years-old, and the days were only too numerous. The Uinta Mountains in the horizon reminded him vaguely of the Caucasus of his youth. Several times a day he would contemplate their eroded profile.

In time he began spending his weeks off with a Ute Indian by the name of Sam Talltree. They would drive aimlessly around the mountain roads in the still-working but spluttering Pontiac, find a nice spot and drink beer, smoke pot and listen to the radio with the car door open. Sam made his living growing hemp, but nobody, including Jimmy, ever got to see his fields.

'Even the word, American, is a sign of US chauvinism,' Sam burst out one day in the middle of a Kenny Rogers song. 'I mean, Americans are people born anywhere from Canada to Argentina, but oh no, in their, and therefore our, understanding of the word it means a person from the United States of America. What kind of bullshit is that? Am I American? Are you?'

'No,' Jimmy replied, choosing to ignore the rhetorical nature of the questions, 'officially I'm a citizen of the Soviet Union, which is also a misnomer. My family is Kumyk, a small offshoot on the Turkish language tree, but I prefer using geography rather than language to determine origin. I'm from Baku and that makes me a Bakunian.'

'Yes, or merely an Asian the same way I'm an American,' Sam stated.

'Yep, Asian, or Caucasian or Azerbaijani. You're a thousand-generation American, a Utah from the reservation more precisely,' Jimmy went on, gesturing vaguely in the direction of the dry plains of the Indians.

'My people were deported here one hundred years ago, but fuck that; I'm still not a real American. I'm a Native American Indian.'

After a short period of silence Jimmy responded to Sam's musings with a Hollywood style war cry, then ventured, 'You rolling another one?'

One day he literally tripped over an edition of the collected poems of Emily Dickinson. A neighbour in the oil workers' residential block had used the small, fat, hardcover book as a doorstopper; Jimmy had skidded on it, and his fall had loosened its cover. Still wincing with pain, he found a scrap of duct tape to repair the book because, in spite of the circumstances, this was too cruel a fate, even for poetry, which he had always considered to be either the anaemic outpourings of navel-gazing weaklings, or vacuous, excessive praise of nature or people in power, but when he glanced at the raw stanzas of this Amherst spinster something strange happened. That same evening he read all 1,775 poems and repeated this the following week. During his second reading he viewed the poems through the lens of death, and, as a consequence, often had to swallow twice, for instance at poem no. 80:

> Our lives are Swiss
> So still – so Cool –
> Till some odd afternoon
> The Alps neglect their Curtains
> And we look farther on!
>
> *Italy* stands the other side!
> While like a guard between –
> The solemn Alps –
> The siren Alps
> Forever intervene!

I want to be able to write like that, Jimmy thought and grabbed a pen, only to suffer an instant attack of writer's block. I need to read more, he decided, and ordered most of what the library service offered by way of 'poetry'. On going through the two small piles he realised that most of it was hogwash. However, a few writers caught his attention, for example Brother Antonius, Gregory Corso and Diane Di Prima, but he was especially moved by the poetry of the Far East as it presented itself to him in two volumes by Kenneth Rexroth: *One hundred poems from the Chinese* (1959) and *One hundred poems from the Japanese* (1964).

Jimmy's interest was also kindled by a book with the simple title *Poems*, composed by one Seymour Glass. The photo on the inside of the jacket showed a man with a large nose, meaty ears and kind eyes. The only information below the photo was the dates 1917–1948.

The poems, numbered 1 to 184, were all a type of double haiku – that is, six lines of verse with thirty-four syllables in total, often, but not always, divided into two stanzas of three lines with the following number of syllables 5-7-5/5-7-5. Glass's slender stanzas were immensely elegant in a very Japanese-Chinese way, but yet radically *twentieth-century American*.

The rhythm and behaviour of the haiku form, almost like the breathing of a small animal, seemed to Jimmy an accessible format, and after a winter

46

spent reading Basho, Issa and his other heroes, and tinkering every evening with his newfound form of expression, he produced two poems, which pleased him:

> The wind turns pages
> in the book one of us left
> on the garden chair

And:

> One appears to hear
> the refrigerator's hum
> just before it stops

Only one adhered to the rule of stating the season, but Jimmy felt that the differences between a haiku in Japanese and one in (American) English, respectively, were so fundamentally profound as to render any comparison meaningless, hence it was preferable to cultivate the English haiku for its own sake. He attempted the Glassian double haiku; however, the form denied him access, the two stanzas slamming shut like an oyster. It was all very mysterious: he was able to compose two haiku on roughly the same subject, but never a double poem whose parts formed a whole. It was as if the young, late Seymour Glass had shut the door behind him as he left.

Over time his 'Jimmy' identity had practically replaced 'Djamolidine', or rather Джамолъдин. His original material had been melted down and poured into a new mould. Jimmy, a first-generation American, had swelled up inside the sack of skin which used to be the Soviet citizen, Djamolidine. All the way to the tips of his fingers. Almost making a small plop sound, he thought. He never spoke Azerbaijani or Russian now; since his arrival in the US he had not missed his racing bike, and his mania for reeling off or listing items had, if not disappeared, then been allocated an appropriate parking space in the periphery of his consciousness. Gradually he became more normal and more American.

One morning in April 1973 he awoke with the certain knowledge of having dreamt in English.

'May I take your coat, sir?' was the question he put to a two-metre-tall rabbit wearing a dinner jacket jumping towards him in a desert where he stood desperate for a drink of water.

'Certainly not, you filthy human!' the rabbit

replied, rapping Jimmy's knuckles with his cane, whose knob, he noticed, was made of cut glass.

Then he woke up with aching fingers.

In biological terms an organism never exists as an isolated phenomenon, but must be understood as a function that resolves the issue of survival of a particular species in time and space. Structure, function and life conditions are symbiotic and evolve in an ever-changing game, like nature's never-ending game of patience, where basic forms and materials have created diversity of the species through simple variation. Certain patterns repeat, for instance blood plasma, nerve cells, enzymatic digestion systems, eyes with pupils and retina, etc. All mammals have fur and three separate auditory ossicles in the air-filled middle ear, and all, except primates, have their shoulder blades either side of their ribcage. All mammals, birds and reptiles – with the exception of snakes, who have lost their limbs in the course of evolution – are tetrapods. This is a basic form which has proven itself to be particularly effective whether movements are quadru- or bipedal, as four-legged creatures have been able to use their front limbs for taking in food, defending themselves, digging etc., while the upright walk of the two-legged ones has freed up their front extremities and allowed them to evolve either into wings or arms with hands, and furthermore, in the case of *Homo sapiens*, with opposing thumbs protruding from a saddle-shaped root joint. The thumb is a precondition for man's undoubted, if somewhat brief, evolutionary success, as his brain expanded in parallel with the increase in possibilities offered by this versatile digit. Our two hands, including our thumbs and their interaction, thus constitute the basic element of what it means to be a functioning human being, which is why the industrial accident that occurred on the 9th of May 1973 robbed Jimmy not only of half his arm, but also his functionality and hence, in a wider context, his existence.

The fatal steel wire, which supported the eight-inch pipeline at Walker Hollow, consisted of nine twisted bundles, each made up of nine smaller bundles, which were each constructed from three individual steel wires. One of these wires had a manufacturing defect, which, once the wire was mounted and suspended on the 7th of February 1953 and subjected to constant tension, provided a mathematical calculation of the date when it would eventually break. Ten years, one month and nineteen days passed before steel wire number two snapped. After another five years and twenty-five days a third wire went and two years, six months and fourteen days later it was the end of number four. This process followed a curve of acceleration and after 7,396 days, on the 9th of May 1973, the last of the 243 wires finally snapped.

Unfortunately Jimmy was leaning his outstretched arm against the pipeline at the very second when the severance process reached its final point. A few moments before, he had become aware of tiny harp-like sounds from the now rapidly snapping steel wires; he had turned his gaze towards the source of the sound and grasped just a second too late what was about to happen. The wire swiped through the air and tore off his arm just above his elbow with such force that the severed arm spun through the air and left circular traces of scarlet blood on the dry ground. Jimmy, at the mercy of gravity and hypovolemic shock, collapsed against the pipeline.

Simultaneously, a few millimetres from the place where his blood coloured the metal pipes warmed by the sun, our drop of oil rushed past him inside the pipeline on its way to the refinery in Salt Lake City, where, after time spent in a crude-oil tank, it would undergo first an atmospheric and later a vacuum distillation. At 165° Celsius the majority of what was once the horse's heart separated from the rest of the crude oil in the form of heavy naphtha and was taken via an ingenious system of pipes to the desulphurisation plant, where catalytic hydrogenation removed hydrogen sulphide from the now paler, but still cloudy liquid. The next step in the refining process was reconstitution in a heated hydrogen atmosphere over a catalyst of platinum and rhenium, which converted the naphthas to aromates, and some of the paraffins to isoparaffins, while the heavier paraffins were broken down into smaller molecules, thus increasing the octane count. And so yet another link was added to the chain of transformation that the heart of the horse had undergone: the state of petrol.

After a long time spent in 10,000-gallon storage tanks, the petrol was drawn off to a tank truck and distributed to a range of petrol stations. Our drop ended up, via various detours, at an Amoco petrol station in Austin, Texas, where it managed a couple of days rest in an underground, concreted-in container before, via pipes and a petrol pump, it ended up in the petrol tank of a Ford Pinto.

This occurred on the 23rd of June 1975. The hand holding the handle of the petrol nozzle and the gaze which absentmindedly followed the small revolving counters on the petrol pump, both belonged to a young woman by the name of Clarissa Sanders. The car belonged to her parents.

The Pinto was a nice, small, subcompact, cheap and streamlined model, which appealed to the American consumer. It had only one flaw: a rear collision at 30 mph or above was likely to cause the petrol tank to explode. The Ford Motor Company discovered the fault before the car was launched in 1970, but it was at that point already in the process of constructing assembly lines and it was consequently deemed unprofitable to alter the design. A cost–benefit analysis was carried out which showed that it was cheaper to pay compensation for 180 fatalities and 180 injured than to fit the petrol tank with one of several possible safety precautions. In the following years Ford lobbied fiercely to prevent the implementation of the Auto Vehicle Safety Act, which would have forced them to modify the Pinto.

At the time when Clarissa was absentmindedly filling up her car, concepts such as 'moderate speed rear-end collision' and 'fuel-fed fire' were unknown to her. Mark Dowie's exposure in *Mother Jones Magazine* was still two years away, and the recall of over 1.5 million cars would not occur for another year after that. What she was wondering about, however, was a smell she recognised, but could not remember why. It came from a tube of sun block she had found in the glove compartment: 'Sun-block on a stick!!!' The three exclamation marks formed the rays of a small sun. The very second she took the cap off the stick a childhood memory of some sort overwhelmed her.

Clarissa Sanders was twenty-two years old, the daughter of a physics teacher and a nurse, and born and bred in Austin, Texas where she was now a second-year biology student. She regarded herself as more or less average: not stupid, but no genius either, neither ugly nor particularly attractive, below average height, mousy brown hair and her breasts an unremarkable B cup. She did not share the interests of other young people of her generation such as rock music, politics or personal development; biology, however, was to her a source of constant fascination. Simultaneously the hippie obsession with nature irritated her exceedingly: holding up a (misunderstood) concept such as 'nature' as an ideal for humanity was, she thought, at the very least profoundly naïve and probably dangerous. Our evolutionary success depends specifically on the brain and the product of it, civilisation, if civilisation is indeed a counter-concept to nature. Clarissa simply had no truck with their argument, as our concepts of nature, civilisation, human beings and animals are so distorted that they must be excluded as useful role models to emulate. Humans themselves are animals, and thus subject to the Darwinist reality: survival of the fittest. At the same time she wondered if this phrase was not indeed a tautology, given that the survivors would always be deemed the fittest, and because it is difficult to measure ability according to anything other than survival.

Anyway, the hippie fantasy of being at one with nature was most charitably regarded as harmless talk, but could – and would theoretically, Clarissa thought, if nature had its way – lead to a regression to primate family herds and ultimately to a configuration of human society along the same model as the naked mole-rat, *Heterocephalus glaber*, one of the mole species that lives in families of fifty to three hundred individuals and spends its entire life in underground tunnel systems. Only one large and aggressive female, the queen, gives birth to the young. She suppresses the sexually active cycles of the other females with pheromones, and permits only one to three of the males to mate with her and inhabit the central chamber where the young are also cared for. The individual naked mole-rat colonies are isolated, as a result of which inbreeding is widespread. This was how any society imitating nature would end up. No, Clarissa thought, nature must be studied because it will further our civilisation. Any understanding of our behaviour should therefore be achieved through controlled experiments in a sterile laboratory; the very opposite of pseudo free love and badly tuned guitar strumming around a campfire.

This spring term she had taken a course in molecular genetics. In her opinion the discovery of the double helix of the DNA molecule had to be the scientific achievement of the century. Moon landings and hydrogen bombs, who cared? Genetics would have the greatest impact on any future society. Once the techniques had been mastered, which for now were mere ideas, it would be possible to eliminate a range of hereditary diseases and minor, as well as major, deformities – but the methods could also be applied to further the improvement of embryos. The augmentation of various physiological aspects, muscle strength, cardiovascular capacity etc., was one option, but it might also be possible to increase logical, deductive, musical or empathetic abilities, for example – and when these generations of super humans began their own research and inventions, their minds would know few limits. That was what she imagined. As she stood there filling up the car with petrol the words 'Above us only sky' and their accompanying melody surfaced in her mind. Her consciousness had long drifted from the smell of the sun block and it was not until the petrol started splashing down onto the tarmac that she became aware of her lack of concentration.

Having paid for the petrol and her regular soda, Mountain Dew, she headed on south. Not that she was going anywhere in particular; she was just passing the afternoon driving. A little later she turned off onto Interstate Highway 35 to San Antonio. At the foot of the access road was a hitchhiker whom she picked up on impulse. He was skinny, with a sallow complexion, and dressed a little shabbily. He also had no lower right arm, something Clarissa only noticed when he stuck out his left hand towards her, and twisted it in order to reach her right one, saying: 'Hi, I'm Jimmy.'

In terms of logic, coincidence is a property or an incident whose existence can be denied without this being a contradiction. According to Aristotle coincidence is a random property, as opposed to a given quantity, which exists independently; that is, it has substance and/or essence. The random element is one of the properties of the substance, which does not form part of its definition and thus does not presuppose its existence. Epistemologically a random sequence of events may be determined by a cause; however, these elude scientific recognition. At the same time they are evidence that all sequences of events are subject to the law of coincidence, given that every single one of the countless events in the universe originates from the very first coincidence, which ripped the nothingness prior to the Big Bang out of its original stability. Or what?

Please would you, dear reader, at this point be so good as to turn back to the beginning of this book and find the word 'somehow' in the third line of the second paragraph? This diffuse adverb carries in the three tiny bellies of its consonants not just the aforementioned coincidence, but also a last hideout for none other than God himself. Because how did this bubble come about? Why was this crushed together space-time unstable? Why is there now something rather than nothing? Science says: because of an impurity in nothingness – a trace element, a ripple – a submicroscopic spot appeared in infinity. But it cannot explain how or why, and thus a vacuum arose for the very human urge to invent a god who can endow man's inexplicable existence with a gloss coat of sense. So this is what the once Almighty Creator has been reduced to: a random impurity in the void. Accident, not substance. And certainly not essence.

'Accident,' was Jimmy's brief answer when Clarissa enquired about his missing arm.

'Not Vietnam?'

'No.'

Whereupon they drove on in silence. The motorway continued in an almost straight line. It was already conspicuous, they both thought, that neither of them had mentioned where they were going. Finally Jimmy made the first move. Her reply with its related counter-question came promptly: 'I don't know. Where are you going?'

'Don't know either. Don't really care anyway. Just travelling,' he replied.

After a short pause she said: 'That's good.'

'That neither of us knows where we want to go?'

'Yes.'

Another silence. Soon the town turned into billboards and industrial areas, which again turned into fruit plantations, wheat fields and more billboards. Clarissa turned on the car radio and after some white noise found a station playing jazz music. A little later, even before the last chord had faded away completely, a speaker's voice burst through with the familiar phrase: 'And now a word from our sponsors. Don't go away.'

Because of the curve in the road Clarissa needed to concentrate on her driving and so she asked Jimmy to find another radio station, which he was busy doing when she said: 'I never buy any products they advertise, because advertising costs money and they can only get that from one source: us, the consumers. Ergo, they add the cost of that to the price of the products. Ergo, the products are overpriced. QED.'

Jimmy glanced sideways at the canned drink in the drinks holder. She noticed his look and explained:

'They hardly ever advertise Mountain Dew. Not like they do with Coke.'

'Okay. But then what would I know? I've only been in the US a few years.'

Clarissa who had noticed his accent, which gave him away as a foreigner straight away, now asked: 'Oh, and where are you from?'

Whereupon he gave her a broad outline of his life story.

Most of her life, that is since she watched a friend being killed in a road accident when she was seven years old, Clarissa had been scared of dying. During puberty this had been combined with a fear of going insane, when an older cousin had been sectioned and she had read a book about psychiatry as a result. Fear and attraction are intimately connected, and the fact that she accepted the tiny square of blotting paper which Jimmy held out to her should thus be attributed to the paradoxical ways in which human beings, precisely because of this fact, tend to act. She was perfectly aware of what it was and had actually had no intention of ever taking it. There were plenty of well-documented cases of psychoses. However, on this day already characterised by impulsive gestures, she continued the pattern by responding to his offer with the words: 'Why not, there's a first time for everything.'

Whereupon she held the steering wheel with one hand and, as her pulse accelerated, followed his lead and picked up the second tiny paper square from his palm with a moist fingertip.

The poisonous ergot, *Claviceps purpurea*, which in cold and damp years grows on rye and barley in particular, is chemically speaking incredibly complex. The sclerotia, the horn-shaped purple bodies of the fungus, contain secale-alkaloids from which a range of medicines have been extracted – for instance, ergotamine for migraines, methyl ergotamine for post partum haemorrhages and bromocriptine for Parkinson's disease. However, the real claim to fame of this tiny fungus is a chemical compound, which Albert Hofmann in 1938 at Sandoz Pharmaceutical Laboratories in Basel produced as the twenty-fifth in a series of partly synthetic lysergic acid amines. Apart from the expected uterotonic effect, he detected no remarkable properties in the substance, which was shelved until one spring day in 1943 when Hofmann decided to examine it more closely and thus prepared a new quantity of LSD-25.

In the course of his work he may accidentally have splashed some of the solution on his fingers, or perhaps he wiped the corners of his mouth. Whichever it was, a strange feeling of restlessness and mild dizziness then forced him to stop work. He went home and experienced a trip of approximately two hours' duration. Hofmann quite rightly attributed this peculiar disturbance to exogenous poisoning and suspected lysergic acid. Three days later he carried out an experiment on himself and administered – in his own view – an absolutely minute dose of 0.25 milligrammes dissolved in tartaric acid. However, the hallucinogenic effect of LSD is almost unbelievably potent: five to 10,000 times stronger than mescaline (which offers the same experience in terms of quality) and Hofmann had consequently, despite his caution, taken at least five times the effective oral dose. That even such a minute amount of LSD has such a potent effect on the human psyche is, as Hofmann himself notes in his book *LSD – mein Sorgenkind* (1970), of great scientific interest: 'With LSD a substance was discovered which, although not naturally occurring in the human body, shows by its existence and effect that abnormal metabolic products, even in trace quantities, might cause mental disturbances. Thus, the opinion that certain mental illnesses have biochemical causes gained further support.'

At a biochemical level it has been established that LSD (lysergic acid diethylamide) interacts with a series of serotonin receptor subtypes (5-HT), primarily in the limbic system, but also in the hippocampus and the hypothalamus – but precisely how and which of the influences determine the hallucinogenic effect is uncertain. The increased presence of serotonin's primary metabolite, hydroxyindoleacetic acid, suggests an increase in the production of this transmitter substance. LSD is probably a potent 5-HT_2 receptor-antagonist, but in addition shows agonistic activities in 5-HT_{IA} and 5-HT_{IC} receptors, which might turn out to be of primary relevance for the effect, given that a number of substances with an antagonistic effect on the central 5-HT_2 receptors are non-hallucinogenic. By means of electroencephalography a generalised excitation of the central nervous system can be seen, and from a physiological point of view there is an increase of activity in the sympathetic nervous system accompanied by a slight rise in body temperature, a faster pulse, higher blood pressure, dizziness and dilated pupils. The effect varies strongly according to dosage, a person's body weight, and, presumably, susceptibility.

Clarissa and Jimmy became aware of the stomach-tingling sensation almost simultaneously; they had each taken a whole tab, but by chance the drop which had been absorbed by his square of paper measured 0.43 microlitre, whereas hers was only 0.36, a variance which was cancelled out by their bodyweights of sixty-seven and fifty-six kilos respectively. At his suggestion she took the next exit and they found a lay-by with a table, benches and a barbeque, all of them concrete, and a swing, a seesaw, and a drinking water fountain. A cluster of pine trees provided the shade.

'Perfect,' he said as she turned off the engine, and by chance she was thinking of the exact same word. The drop, which had once been the heart of a horse, splashed around in the petrol tank.

From the outside there were no discernible changes except their laughter which constantly bubbled up through a pretend suppression and they interrupted themselves frequently and for longer and added a lethargy to their actions which translated into their body language as they emptied out his rucksack looking for chocolate or perhaps some nuts which soon became irrelevant anyway as this magic bag contained random objects revealing profound stories about themselves and indirectly their owner and much later when every object discovered had been placed in lines as straight as an arrow on the concrete table she surveyed them and felt that she possessed a knowledge of him which exceeded what any biography could provide as insight could be gained through objects but what are things he asked her and together they explored the limits of the world of objects by looking into each others eyes and around the lay-by until their investigation focused on the drinking fountain with its life-giving fluidum which is also an object even though water is a liquid or that is to say so is steam and ice snow hailstone fog and the water in our bodies whereupon they returned to the table and the objects on display which they in their individual ways examined his old trousers red plastic lunchbox with transparent lid sunglasses the folder with the greyhound bus timetable but not the notebook which had burned in her hand the very first time it appeared from the magic bag and now lay in serene silence and mild closure and she was not going to and everything was fine that way that he said there is nothing there and she well there must be something he sure but nothing of interest not even for me i never read what i once wrote it served a purpose at the time and cleared my head but the object of writing on the page is a by-product just leftovers and if i happen one day to be leafing through it and here his breathing made a strange rasping noise an old note-book it is like seeing embarrassing photos where you are drunk and gross at some party that you now only recall on account of something stupid you said to someone who was important in those days and it is vital they told each other to keep the focus on a given action or train of thought gratifying your needs experiences or mere sentence for continuously over-turned detours and sidelines just cross them and when they tried to get back to the main track that too turned out to be a diversion just an older one perhaps several hours and they found her watch and not even one hour had passed since time had started to swell up in their heads and they gave each moment their complete attention and all the time responded with a pliable elasticity in a rhythm of tension and relaxation and again as the secondhand pushed its way around the dial as if moving through jelly rather than air not stopping for an instant even though she felt that every single tick had to be the last one but every time the hand overcame the resistance and shifted at the very last moment and she looked up again he had gone back to the car and the sight of his half arm inside the shirtsleeve with a knot tied at the end made her remember that she had been allowed to touch but then it struck her that this remembered touch was surely just a memory of an imagined touch when he in response to her question had shown her his arm stump but even that she was no longer sure of and at the same time a bird flew past at low height she ducked as he turned on the car radio and angry guitar music poured out and when she thought of asking him to turn it off he did and left the car with the door open and started out on the vast journey to the water fountain and she followed and they got their hair wet and felt it dry and saw patterns in the steam and the sun caught in the floating water throwing barely visible prisms of some similarity to thoughts he imagined and said so and then she was thinking the same and soon they had reached a new ants nest under the table they live on crumbs and garbage he said they get their water from over there she added

pointing to the water fountain the trees too live off
the spilt water and so it was and he talked about a
zarathustrian shrine in iran where a single drop
constantly drips from a mountain side and feeds a
huge pale green cluster of plants and being an
ordinary american she has only the vaguest ideas of
zarathustrians and iran but she did not have the
energy to ask as the implications of structuring a
sentence grew exponentially and left her hanging on
an arbitrary branch weightless happily lost and fully
aware of the chemical basis of her condition plus
where she was and what she was doing nothing
mysterious there then she visualised the pattern of
his iris and asked to see it again and she remembered rightly that there was a circular marking in
his left eye paler in the dark brown with offshoots
to both sides to the right down towards the nose
the lines spread out into a triangle and the whole
composition looked like a trumpet or perhaps a
postman's bugle perhaps with the corner of his eye
acting as a muffler she thought an entire jazz
orchestra behind his forehead and the music poured
out of his mouth he was singing and then said that
it was an old russian melody and gestured towards
the dry slopes as far as the eye could see she looked

at him once more and gave him an imaginary kiss
and reached the conclusion no mainly because the
hyper complex motor skills required to carry out
such an act exhausted her in advance as she had to
have herself present in every single movement there
was no other way in this state the task would grow
outside her control so she chose not to and outlined
the contours of the slopes with her finger in the air
accompanied by a whistling corresponding in pitch
and then he wanted to eat and opened his lunchbox
again and took one of the sandwiches ham cheese
tomato and gave it to her and sunk his teeth into
the other one straight away followed by energetic
munching and she turned her attention to this peculiar edibility which took on a wealth of detail the
closer she looked and the urge to eat was far removed
from her or rather beyond her capability it was too
complicated as everything ultimately is and suddenly
the light changed as a small cloud blocked out the
sun and the light behind this elevated lump of mois-
ture made it beautiful but it was not an hallucina-
tion she knew that and did not need to remind
herself to be constantly present in the patient enthu-
siastic churning of her consciousness.

*   *   *

A small eternity later, descending from the altitude of the trip, they got ready to leave the lay-by. However, they still did not know where to go. He was standing by the passenger door, she by the driver's door as they talked across the roof of the car.

'Where did you come from?' he asked, attempting to reverse the logic. 'Perhaps you need to go back to your starting point in order to know where you want to go?'

'That's a bit feeble, don't you think? Surely all you'll learn is where you wanted to go at that time. Besides 'my starting point', where is that? When I got out of bed this morning? The hospital where I was born? The country my ancestors came from? And which ancestors? The apes?'

Jimmy's only response to this cascade of questions was a defensive half-grunt. Then he had an idea. 'Let me drive.'

'You want to drive? With one arm?'

'I only need one hand for steering.'

'How about changing gears? It's a stick-shift.'

'I'll need your help there. I'll let you know when I put down the clutch.'

'Okay.'

They walked around the car, and at the tip of the

bonnet, where more luxurious models display an insignia, their elbows brushed against each other. They got in. He adjusted the seat and the mirrors, put down the clutch and reached over with his left arm to turn the key in the ignition. She put the car into first gear. He turned his attention to the area delineated by the windows and mirrors and started driving.

Once the engine had settled into fourth gear Clarissa said: 'When I was a child I used to imagine that if aliens were watching the earth from outer space they would think that the planet was ruled by a strange species called cars. Most of them have four wheels, but there are much bigger beasts with up to twelve giant wheels and smaller creatures with only two. The cars are served by two-legged, smaller animals that spend their lives waiting on them; the cars need regular feeding with liquid food and must be healed after illnesses and accidents; the two-legged slave animals assist even when cars are born or when they die and they are kept in cages next to the cars, so they're ready to accompany the cars whenever they want to go somewhere new. The slave animals build and service complex networks of roads, which allows the cars to move unhindered from place to place.'

It had quickly become superfluous to mention when the gears needed changing; she listened out for differences in the engine sounds and could tell from the state of the traffic whether the gears would need to go up or down.

Then he said: 'Maybe that's how it is: cars control the world, and we, their slaves in our cages, just don't know it.'

She did not reply immediately, but was silent for a while and then she suggested: 'Perhaps we should drive back to my cage in Austin. At least there'll be tea and probably some bread or biscuits.'

'Super,' said Jimmy and prepared to turn the car around. On their way back to the city, Clarissa told him about the glorious future which she believed gene manipulation techniques would bring. When he had finally understood what she was talking about, Jimmy countered: 'But don't you think these glorious possibilities will be available to the rich only? With the introduction of gene technology the gap between the haves and the have-nots can only widen; indeed it will be possible to tell if a person belongs to the upper or the lower class purely from their body. Once upon a time it would be calloused hands that gave away the farmer or the worker. In your version of the future, we'll be able to spot the poor because they wear glasses, are less than six feet tall or have other minor physical flaws. It's going to be one ugly world.'

'What are you, a Communist?' Clarissa asked sceptically.

'No I'm not, and certainly not in the Soviet sense of the word. I believe in the freedom of the individual. That's what you have here in the US, but I believe that poverty and racism will ultimately cause the system to break down from the inside, though I accept that it will take time. The materialistic escapism of the white middle classes seemingly knows no bounds, and that is why the inertia of the system can be sustained for a very long time.'

'You *are* a Communist,' she declared. 'You ought to love your adopted country.'

'Again no, and yes I do. "I pledge allegiance to the flag . . ." and all that and that is precisely why it pains me to see my newly adopted country head for its downfall. On the other hand: everything moves towards its own destruction; all empires collapse eventually. It shouldn't come as a surprise.'

She jerked her head a little and proceeded to change the subject by enquiring as to his current occupation.

He replied: 'Nothing, just drifting. I get a small pension from my work injury. I used to drive around in a Pontiac, but it broke down.'

It was almost 8 p.m. on the 23rd of June 1975 when our drop of fuel, which was once the heart of a horse, exploded in the third cylinder in the Kent engine of the Pinto 1.6L. It happened as they turned right into the car park at Timber Creek Apartments: the fibres in the calf muscle of Jimmy's right leg had reacted to the electrochemical signals from his nervous system with a contraction that rearranged the internal positioning of the ankle bones, thus creating a downward pressure which transmitted through his sock and shoe to the rubber-covered surface of the accelerator pedal. From the pedal the command was transmitted to the throttle valve, which opened up and activated the fuel injection system, thus sucking the drop from the tank and transporting it via the pump to the filter and from there into the carburettor that mixed the fuel with air from the open throttle valve. The mixture was carried through the suction manifold to the injection nozzle of the third cylinder, where the suction valve opened as the piston moved downwards from its uppermost dead centre and created a subpressure which sucked the aerated petrol into the cylinder. At the lowest dead centre of the piston, the valve closed so the piston, returning to its upper dead centre, compressed the gas mixture, and just before its arrival the spark plug gave off a tiny spark and ignited the petrol whose combustion occurred at a temperature of just below 2000° Celsius and a pressure of 40 bar.

'BANG!' it went.

Simultaneously as the liquid and the gas were converted into plasma, a veritable infinity of other events occurred inside the car as well as to the car itself. For example, at this very moment Clarissa made a life-changing decision. When she was a little girl her mental picture of a crazy person was a kind of romantic madman-stroke-genius: Beethoven as a tramp, the visionary truth teller who has seen through the pretence of 'normal' society and responds with flights of fancy, inappropriate laughter and a lonely toast in cherry brandy. However, at some point, triggered by a cousin's illness she read a library book: Stafford-Clark's *Psychiatry Today* from 1961, where she learned that mental disorders are genuine illnesses with painful symptoms, not a free choice made by elevated people. Reading this book instilled in her a fear that became an almost constant companion in her waking hours – and oddly only then: her dreams were remarkably peaceful; she hardly ever suffered from nightmares. Away from the embrace of sleep, however, she was alone with her fear. All the way through high school, and even today for that matter, she had been waiting for her debut as a schizophrenic. Now, at the very same second as our drop of petrol, which had once been the heart of a horse, exploded, she asked herself entirely without prejudice for the first time the ultimately very simple question: 'Why don't I just drop it?'

At the very same moment the phantom pains in Jimmy's arm hit the crest of their wave. The fatal steel wire had amputated his lower arm, but not the corresponding parts of his motor and sensory cortex. The cerebral image of his body was thus intact and the lesions in the peripheral nervous system occasionally triggered erroneous transmissions to the nociceptive paths and subsequently he experienced tightening, pulsating and stinging pains in the missing arm. These symptoms had subsided considerably a few months after the accident and stabilised at a level where they only made themselves known a few times every day, though more frequently when he was performing an activity where his right hand should have been involved, such as now when he was driving a car. But instead of his sinewy Caucasian hand, it was her small Caucasian fingers closing round the black knob of the gear stick. An image of pain as dark stormy weather with tiny flashes of lightning, her fingers representing goodness and beauty, passed in front of his mind's eye.

This moment also included a violent death, which took place less than one metre from the tips of their noses. An autumn fly, *Musca autumnalis*, got smeared against the windscreen of the car just above the left windscreen wiper. It was a young female who had crawled out from a cowpat that very morning and was now eagerly buzzing around without remembering her larval state and thus never having to forget it; she was busy trying out her crisp new wings when her rear body was forced through her head. Jimmy saw the small dark red spot appear and wondered whether to switch on the windscreen wipers.

Measured doses of dry desert air filled the car through the air conditioning system, which was set at the first of its four levels and directed at the upper bodies of the passengers. The few litres of air that at this time were passing through the system contained thousands of floating particles, including a double digit number of spores of the fungus *Ganoderma lucidum*, best known by its Chinese name, Lingshi, or its Japanese one, Reishi. The actual fungi, which these spores originated from, were descendants of fungi introduced by Chinese railway workers in the 1860s.

The centrifugal force inside the car created by the right-hand turn caused the sun stick in the glove compartment to roll to the left until it was stopped by a folder of stiff, dark blue plastic, which contained a road map of the state of Texas, published by Lone Star State maps. It was a complimentary map, which had been given to Clarissa's mother when she bought the car nearly two years ago, and it had only been taken out of its plastic folder once when the dealer had shown it to her. In addition, the glove compartment contained a scrunched up chewing-gum wrapper, an invoice from Johnston Motor Repairs to the tune of $4.95, a black ballpoint pen, a pair of tweezers and a nail file, plus a child's drawing depicting a house, a tree and a black bird with bloodshot eyes. The same red colour had been used for the angular signature 'Jennifer'.

The radio had been turned off and neither of them

spoke; there was silence inside the car, but the small space was nevertheless penetrated by a vast number of electromagnetic waves: various AM and FM wavelength radio stations, TV-signals from twenty-three different channels, microwaves, radar, X-ray, gamma and heat radiation together with visible light, and all of them, with the exception of the last, went more or less directly through the passengers and the car.

Subconscious processes triggered by the fly splattering on the windscreen caused Jimmy's saliva secretion to increase. His parasympathetic nervous system had passed a command on to the muscle-like structures surrounding his salivary glands, which, thus stimulated, released their mixture of water, mucus and mucines. The saliva also contained basic substances such as chlorides, phosphates and bicarbonates in concentrations matching those of the blood. In addition to those there were enzymes such as ptyalin which breaks down starch, and lysozyme which kills bacteria. However, as there was no food in Jimmy's mouth, the unused saliva ended up gliding down the darkness of his throat.

Clarissa turned her eyes in the direction of driving. The photoreceptors of her retinas adjusted to the distance, the light etc. and sent their images, converted into neurochemicals, to her occipital lobe from where they were dispatched for interpretation by the relevant areas of the brain, which, without any difficulties, found a template that matched her visual impression: the car park outside her apartment block.

Thousands of sand and dust particles that over time had accumulated in every nook and cranny of the car, underneath the windscreen wipers, around the headlights, the radiator grille, the doors etc. were also affected by the centrifugal force of the turn and formed new, fleeting patterns. One particular ovoid grain of sand – an oolith as it is known: concentrically precipitated calcium carbonate surrounding a quartz grain barely half a millimetre in length – had been stuck to the underside of the car for months, trapped by a smidgen of oil. The history of the oolith stretches far back to a fiery inferno 1.6 billion years ago, and continued to unfold at a lake shore in the Permian period 250 million years ago, but as this grain of sand plays only a minor role in our story, that is all I'm going to say on that subject. The wind had slowly moved it from the petrol tank, across the rear axle and the differential housing, to the exhaust pipe where it was now being torn from the mouth of the pipe in a filament of oil.

The majority of the soot particles that swirled around the portion of exhaust gas fumes, which had once been the heart of a horse, were compressed into a small constellation which was snapped up by the greasy oolith at the mouth of the exhaust pipe. A little later this small assemblage of grain of sand, oil and exhaust particles loosened itself from the pipe and was carried by the wind up to a height of twenty metres. Having ascended for a fair amount of time, then fallen and flown here and there, our little fragment ended up underneath the eaves, where it attached itself to a gangling thread from a long-since-abandoned spider's web. Here it hung for just under twenty-four hours, swaying in the warm, lazy, Texan breeze until a balcony door below was pushed open, thus creating a subpressure wind that ripped the soot particles from the grain of sand, oil and cobweb.

The hand on the balcony door belonged to Clarissa and the scream, which echoed through the trees on the slope a moment later, came from her throat. Its piercing sound stopped me in my tracks as I was playing on the balcony of the neighbouring flat; I was nine years old at the time. As I recall, the scream was entirely devoid of any shades of emotion and lasted for as long as she had sufficient breath.

Afterwards she gasped for air and, apart from her panting, the breeze in the trees was the only sound to be heard. At that moment of near silence Clarissa's fate was sealed as the soot particles of the ex-heart of the horse were caught by one of her forceful inhalations and sucked into the darkness of her lungs.

Cancer is both a slow and a fast-moving disease. The second the carcinogenic agent penetrates the healthy cell, it launches a frenzied attack on the double helix of the hereditary genes, but decades can pass before external symptoms manifest themselves. In Clarissa's case less than one minute passed from when the soot particles hit the inner surface of the bronchiole to when benzapyrene, the carcinogenic agent, buried itself in a specific epithelial cell where it de-programmed the death of the cell, apoptosis, thus rendering the cell immortal – that is, transforming it into a cancer cell. However, thirty whole years would pass until she was diagnosed with 'metastasised adenocarcinoma (stage III)'.

What happened was that she knocked on my door

for the first time after having been my neighbour for all these years. The restraint was not a sign of hostility; as a rule you rarely greeted your neighbours in Timber Creek Apartments with anything more than a silent nod of the head. I did know who she was though. Miss Sanders, laboratory technician at the Department of Biology; after all we had had adjacent balconies for more than thirty years. Through the spyglass I could see that she was holding her hand over her mouth. I opened the door.

'I'm not feeling very well. Please would you drive me to the hospital?' Her voice broke into a cough. A trickle of blood seeped out between her fingers.

'Just a moment,' I said and fetched my car keys, and a packet of paper tissues which I handed to her as we walked across the car park. She coughed up more blood, stumbled, and I had to support her. I eased her into the passenger seat. She was bound to stain the upholstery, but I wasn't bothered about that because, for once, I was doing something motivated by genuine altruism. I was seven months into a depression caused by the realisation of man's total and inescapable selfishness and I'm aware that pedants might argue that I was only driving my neighbour to the hospital in order to avoid a guilty conscience and find myself subjected to condemnation by all and sundry, but at that moment these objections were invalid. The car started without any trouble even though it had sat there unused for weeks.

I drove her to South Austin Hospital at Ben White Boulevard where they asked me to wait. After two hours a nurse appeared and told me that Clarissa Sanders had been admitted, that she (Clarissa) had asked her (the nurse) to thank me and that I was free to go home now.

A week later there was a knock on my door, and again it was Clarissa. She had now been equipped with an oxygen device which she plugged into a socket, having come inside and accepted my offer of a cup of tea. She opened the apparatus: inside hung two small plastic bottles and she tipped a small amount from each of them into a mouthpiece. Then she closed the machine which began emitting a faint humming when she pressed a button, and put on a transparent plastic mask connected to the device via a tube.

After a pause where only the humming of the machine and her breathing could be heard, she pulled the mask down to her chin and said: 'They tell me I've got cancer.'

I replied: 'I'm sorry to hear that.' And not much else happened during this visit.

Three months later she was taken away in an ambulance never to return.

Around that time I had started to frequent a health centre in the Appalachian Mountains, whose facilities included an Indian sweat hut. It is possible that I had entertained a naïve belief that I could force my depression out through the pores of my skin and I had therefore decided to participate in a modified version of a Native American sweat hut ritual.

Including the master of ceremony we were seven people in total going into the hut that day. Inside darkness and silence reigned, but my senses were quickly heightened and I was able to make out the faint, dark red light from the hot stones and the multitude of tiny sounds coming from the participants. The intense heat instantly made you sweat and feel thirsty. The master of ceremony threw a cup of water on the stones, which resulted in a whiplash sound and a wave of steam that smashed against our bodies. We sat in silence in the hot darkness for what I was told afterwards was forty-five minutes.

No book in the world is big enough to contain all

the thoughts you can think in that period of time. My brain exploded with images, feelings and words, mixing them all up as it visited an infinite number of nooks and crannies from my past, my present and my notions of the future, but slowly my inner monologue acquired a sense of direction and headed for the horizon. After a while I was cleansed of irrelevant thoughts and accepted this winding path, which was matched by the sweat trickling down my body. My mental state grew denser, and I had started to wonder if I had actually fainted when I came across a creature which I immediately recognised as my totem animal.

It was a horse, quite a small one, the size of a smallish dog, with grey and brown flecked fur and paws rather than hooves. It was visible in the darkness – not luminous, it was just there. The horse opened its mouth and started talking and I understood everything, even though it wasn't speaking in English or any other human language. The language of the horse was one modulated sound with myriad meanings, associations and overlapping images. In my cleansed and possibly unconscious state, I understood that it was telling me the story of the fate of its heart.

Over the past year I have tried to reconstruct and

translate this wordless equine language, and these pages are the outcome of my efforts. It has been a laborious task, filled with frustration at my many inadequacies, but it has occupied me to such an extent that I, I now realise, have entirely forgotten to be depressed.

Now I will go for a walk by the river.

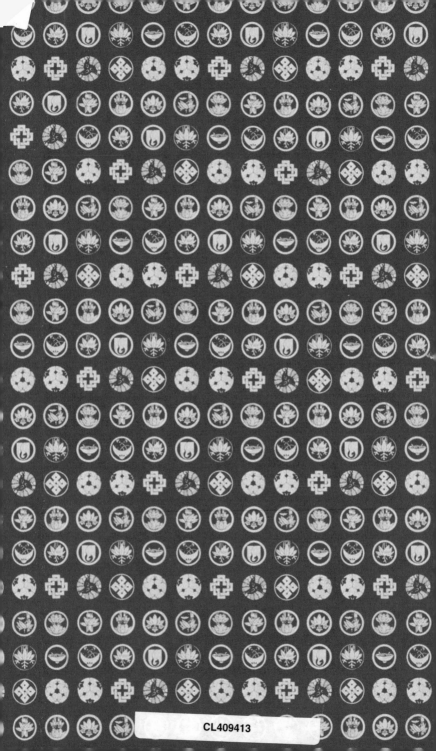